Noodle's Hard Lesson Learned

Noodle's Hard Lesson Learned

The Story of the Mai Family, an Albino Cobra family as they struggle to survive in the jungle in evading predators as their colors makes them visible to their enemies

Antonio Carnovale

iUniverse, Inc.
Bloomington

NOODLE'S HARD LESSON LEARNED
The Story of the Mai Family, an Albino Cobra family as they struggle to survive in the jungle in evading predators as their colors makes them visible to their enemies

iUniverse books may be ordered through booksellers or by contacting:

iUniverse
1663 Liberty Drive
Bloomington, IN 47403
www.iuniverse.com
1-800-Authors (1-800-288-4677)

ISBN: 978-1-4759-9532-9 (sc)
ISBN: 978-1-4759-9533-6 (ebk)

Printed in the United States of America

iUniverse rev. date: 06/13/2013

Table of Contents

Pattaya

Chapter One

Paradise lost

In a land far, far away, called Siam or Thailand, which means "land of the free', there lived a family of rare white albino Cobras (snakes). These Cobras, because of their color were hunted by the other snakes and predatory animals and the very evil and deadly mongoose. Never the less the white cobras lived happily at the edge of the jungle of blackness, which stretched out to meet the carpet of white, which divided the water of salt from the jungle of blackness. Pattaya was a little corner of tranquility in a very real and dangerous world.

You had to be extremely careful in the mid afternoon sun not to step on the Cobras as they enjoyed themselves baking in the sun.

The Pattaya sand was so white and so fine, that it actually gave the white Cobras some camouflage protection from their natural enemies.

The water of salt reached out to embrace the beautiful, mysterious coastline of the Gulf of Thailand; the emerald water of salt was pierced by jagged rocks resembling freckles on natures face. The sun, as if an Aztec medallion of gold, would descend in the west signaling to all living beings that another day's journey had come to its conclusion. A white silvery moon and a sky of dark blue that was decorated by twinkling bright stars would now replace the suns reflection. The life of the jungle seemed to come to life serenading all that would listen, reminding everyone that other creatures were lurking and watching and so it was here that the Mai family lived. Dad was a seven-foot albino cobra named Rama, but called affectionately, Cakes, by his friends. Rama was well liked and was mated to a beautiful six-foot albino cobra named Teo; they had two beautiful strong children, a four-foot teenage boy named Tak, who had been nicknamed Noodles for his long narrow torso. Noodles did not take life very seriously and he never really listened to his parents. Noodles always believed that he knew more than they did. Noodles had a sister named Lek (which means "Little One" in Thai). Lek was about two feet long and was everything that Noodles was not. Lek was obedient, conscientious, and always listened to her parents.

Because of their color, the albino cobras were always bullied, picked on and made fun of because of their white color (white in the snake world is not very well liked).

The Albino Cobras were not able to camouflage themselves in the blackness of the jungle and were always exposed to their enemies. It was very rare when an Albino Cobra lived a full life and here in Pattaya, we had a whole family trying to survive in this corner of Paradise. Noodles and Lek were always made fun of and bullied by the many enemies of the Cobras, but Noodles and Little One ignored the bullying and racial insults as they tried to live a normal life. Cakes and Teo had always taught their children, Noodles and Lek, to respect all life and not to judge others by the color of their scales or skin, but to try to see the inner beauty. They taught them to judge other living creatures by their actions and purity of heart and never live by the old motto, "an eye for an eye and a fang for a fang" because Teo and Cakes would always remind their young Cobras that if everyone lived by that creed that the world would be blind and fangless.

The Mai family, in spite of all the dangers, was as happy as they could be and they could always be found frolicking in the mid afternoon sun of Thailand, sunbathing, enjoying their life while still being aware of their surroundings.

Teo and Rama were always on the lookout for their natural enemies; they worried for their children and were particularly on the lookout for the bad snake catchers who were combing the area for reptiles. These snake hunters could make a lot of money by capturing snakes and then selling these snakes to the snake shows in the big city of Bangkok (the capital of Thailand), Bangkok had traffic, crime and was not a nice place for snakes, and it was far, far away from Pattaya. Bangkok was another world.

Teo and Rama could always be heard instructing their little ones about the dangers of the outside world and in particular, the snake catchers, and the evil mongoose. Teo and Rama always reminded the children to stay close to the nest and not to stray too far and never trust strangers, people, or animals and never, ever take anything from the evil doers who were lurking in every dark area of Pattaya, ready to kidnap young snakes. The parents were also very concerned that the family had very white scales and could not camouflage itself very well in the jungle of blackness, and therefore would be extremely visible to the natural enemies of the Cobras.

Now, Lek was a good obedient daughter who always seemed to listen attentively to her mother and father, but Noodles, oh! Their Noodles, he was a full four feet long, no one would mess with him, Noodles, after all, was a tough cobra. Noodles believed that he could protect himself and never took the warnings of his parents very seriously; after all, he knew that his parents were just trying to scare him.

HOTEL

Noodles was a very curious snake and one morning he decided that he would explore the far side of the beach at Pattaya. Noodles had been told of a beautiful resort called Centare Grande Mirage, but it was quite a good distance from his nest, but Noodles had no fear, after all he was almost four feet long and he knew that he could handle any surprises that would come his way. Noodles was strong, he was quick, agile, fast, and full of spirit, and so what could go wrong?

This morning, Noodles was really curious and anxious to explore the other side of the Pattaya beach and like the forbidden apple, Noodles had to see for himself. Besides, Noodles would be back in plenty of time, what could go wrong? And plus his parents would never even miss him. Tia and Rama would never even know that he was gone, but Noodles conscience kept telling him that he should not stray from their home base. His parents had warned on many occasions about how "curiosity had killed the little cobra," but no matter, Tak had made up his mind to slither away to the far side of Pattaya. Noodles was confident, it would be a short trip, and he would be back soon enough. As he began to slither towards the western outreaches of his destination, using the jungle cover as best as he could for camouflage, it had taken Noodles a little longer to reach his destination. Noodles had also not realized that he had slithered out of the cover of the jungle and into the white sand of the beach, but he thought that was not a problem, as he seemed to blend in with the white color of the sand. However, Noodles was in full site for all to see, that was very dangerous. Noodles was very vulnerable, especially to the snake hunters who were prowling in the area for reptiles. It was at this time that a human female swimmer realized that the sand was moving and upon a closer look, she realized it was a white cobra and she let out a deafening shriek as she yelled "Snake!"

Chapter Two

Captivity

Then all went dark for Noodles, he had become another victim of the snake catchers. Those terrible people had thrown a net over Noodles and the more that he struggled the more he was drawn into the tangled web of a trap. Noodles soon realized that to struggle was useless and soon he gave way to whatever fate might be waiting him. Soon Noodles felt human hands pick him up, how clammy they were, and how smooth, how terrible. It must be awful to be human, Noodles thought. When Noodles could finally see daylight again, he realized that he was in a steel cage with other snakes. Noodles wondered whether he looked as scared as the other snakes in the cage looked. They were all being transported somewhere but somewhere . . . where? Far away from his beloved Pattaya. Noodles kept hearing his parent's warnings. "Noodles stay close to home, don't stray too far from the nest, don't make yourself visible, and don't trust any strangers." Yet here he was alone, scared, sobbing and being driven to a mysterious fate far away from his loving family and his beloved Pattaya. Noodles wondered if he would ever see his family and home again. Oh! How he should have listened to his parents, Oh! God! Please help me escape and I will be the best, the most obedient snake ever.

The ride was bumpy and dusty and after a half a day's ride, the truck came to a stop. The terrible snake catchers with long snake poles with a noose at the end grabbed the snakes one by one and dropped them into a containment area filled with many other snakes. Fear began to grip Noodles as his whole body trembled, shaking uncontrollably. Anger and then resignation engulfed his every being. Noodles was crying when an older snake took pity upon him, his name was Gupta and Gupta approached Noodles. Gupta was wearing glasses and had a white beard and he said, in a very deep voice to Noodles, "Hey, Little cobra, don't cry. I am Gupta from Prechimburi and I have survived the snake catchers and the snake show and if you want to live you must be strong and you must listen to everything that I am going to tell you and follow my advice."

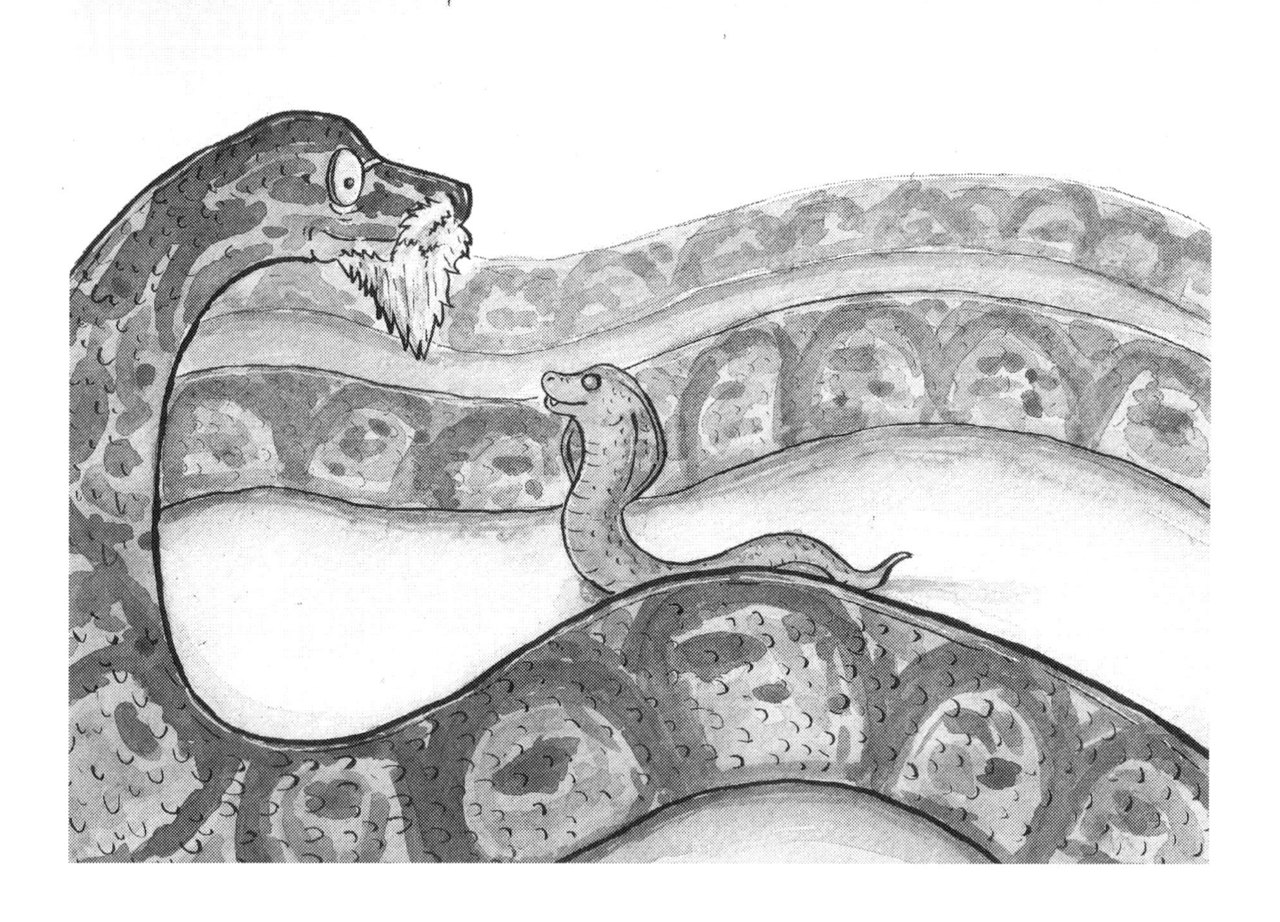

Chapter Three

Wisdom of the Old

Gupta began to explain how he too was caught when he was only eight feet long and at a time in his life when he believed that he knew all the answers. Oh, how a little bit of knowledge is a very dangerous thing and how it got him into trouble! Like Noodles, he had strayed away from home. Gupta too did not listen to his parents, he too had run into the evil snake catchers, and now he was here and five years later and twenty-five feet long. Gupta was in captivity with no hope of seeing his family or his beautiful Prechimburi ever again.

Gupta was getting old and he had realized that he probably would not be able to hunt for food on the outside as he once did. He had lost his hunting skills and was now content to being at the mercy of the snake catcher who would bring him mice, rats and other rodents in order for him to stay alive. All he had to do was let the spectators touch him and have their pictures taken with him. How Gupta disliked the snake catchers. Gupta knew that he had given up of ever returning home, but he was determined to help little Noodles persevere and remain strong and maybe help him escape from this horrible place. As Gupta looked at Noodles, who was trembling, Gupta with a booming voice said, "I will help you escape but you must listen and do exactly as I say, do you understand little one, little white one?" Noodles was still trembling, he was sad, he was scared, but he had been taught to respect older snakes for they were wise beyond their time. As Noodles looked at Gupta, he realized that for the first time, Noodles was not just hearing the words of Gupta, Noodles was really listening. It finally had dawned on him that with time comes knowledge and with age it is accumulated. Through experience, which helps in making the right decisions, using the wisdom and intelligence, which Noodles, had so disregarded all his years, and now he paid particular attention as he wanted to live.

Gupta again began to speak slowly. Choosing his words carefully as he looked Noodles in the eyes and he said, "First beware of the evil Mongoose, he is immune to your venom and cannot be killed by poison. The Mongoose is quick and is a killer of snakes. The Mongoose is the enemy of the Cobras and tomorrow the Mongoose will try to kill you. Tomorrow the snake catchers will put you on display on a stage in the center of a small theatre, a coliseum. You will be surrounded by spectators, and two other brother snakes will be forced to join you on stage. The Mongoose, at some point will enter the stage and at the appropriate moment will strike at you and try to kill you. However, remember that he likes to attack the snake on the right first. Noodles you must try to set yourself up to the Mongoose left and as he lurches forward to his right, then and only then will you have the opportunity to escape. You must be quick, you cannot hesitate and do not look back because the Mongoose could be gaining on you. When you hit the floor, you must slither as quickly as you can to the nearest door, head for the sunlight. A few feet outside you will see the waters of the Chao Phraya River, a tributary of the mother of rivers, the great Mekong. You must jump into the river and go with the flow of the waters; the river flow will take you to the water of salt. Upon tasting salt water, you will be close to home. Leave the water, and then and only then, enter the jungle of darkness and travel towards the setting sun and you will reach Pattaya. You must travel at night, floating down the river and you must hide in the jungle of darkness during the day to avoid predators. Keep your distance from the Mongoose and when you think you cannot go any farther, think of your family for inspiration and you will survive." Noodle listened attentively as he prepared himself mentally for the next day's reckoning.

The caged area that Noodles was kept in was very restrictive; Noodles could only see glimpses of his beloved sun. Oh! How he longed for the sun's rays, to warm his scales again and to bring pleasure to his body once more and never would he take the sun, his freedom, his family for granted again.

It seemed that whenever Noodles moved, he was bumping into other snakes. Some were not so friendly at all, while others were just outright mean. So the time passed, painfully slow as the blanket of night descended on Noodles' little world. Noodles was filled with despair; many negative thoughts entered his head, but he knew that he must preserve and survive if he ever wanted to see his family again. Noodles had prepared himself mentally and he would try to seize the moment and make his escape.

In Pattaya, Teo and Rama (Cakes) had searched far and wide for Noodles and now they were exhausted. Teo wept inconsolably, her little Noodles was missing. Rama had felt despair, but now that despair had given way to alarm. The realization was starting to set in with the Mai family; little Noodles was a prisoner of the snake catchers. Rama was angry. Rama just wanted to lash out at someone, anyone. Rama just wanted to bite someone, and Rama was blaming himself for not keeping a closer eye on Noodles.

During the night, Noodles could hear a high pitched gurgling sound, it was a sound that was chilling and when he asked what that was, Gupta, the old snake, replied, "Little white cobra, that is your worst enemy, that is the killer mongoose, beware . . . beware."

Noodles did not sleep much that night. He was scared of the unknown, but as the sun forced itself upon the dark sky, light began to take hold and a new dawn had approached.

Chapter Four

The Escape

That morning seemed hectic as the snake catchers seemed to move with a sense of urgency. Noodles was placed in a different cage with two other reptiles, small like himself. Noodles knew that the time had come to face the Mongoose. But was he ready? Would Noodles seize the moment? He could hear the noise and the roar of the crowd. Gupta was taken out as the crowd was in awe of the huge Python and now it was his turn. The snake handlers came in, picked up the cage and transported the snakes to the stage in the center of a circular small coliseum, but Noodles felt bad for his two brother snakes and told them what he was going to do and what they should do to survive.

The cage was brought to the stage, the room was full of smoke, the humans were yelling and screaming, and the rays of the sun penetrated the old dilapidated building. The snake handler used long tongs to grab the three snakes and put them on the stage. Noodle was in the middle, he would have even less time to escape from the Evil Mongoose, and now another cage was brought in and there he was, the Mongoose with a small pointed face. Noodles thought he looked like a weasel; he had small ears and somewhat of a long tail and this animal that was immune to my venom was here to kill me. The Mongoose came out of the cage looking confident, he had killed many snakes before, and this was routine for him.

The Mongoose began to stare almost hypnotically at us, I was tense, and without warning, the Mongoose struck the snake to my left and to the Mongoose's right. Just as Gupta, the old wise python had predicted that he would do, I seized the moment and jumped off the stage before I could give the Mongoose the chance to strike at me, the small cobra to my right and the Mongoose to the left followed me from the stage. I headed straight for the door, the other cobra following me and the Mongoose fast on our heels. The humans began to scamper, the human females began to scream as I slithered through the first door and on the way to the second floor. A number of snake catchers reached for us but I was too quick. I reached the second door and I heard the other cobra call out for help, as I turned to look I could see a net covered his body. There was nothing I could do except to keep moving. As I slithered through the second door, I jumped into the Chao Phraya River. The river began to take me down stream at a bend in the river. Noodles left the water in order to hide in the Jungle of Darkness and wait for the cover of night, just as the old python had told him to do and as the darkness descended over Siam, Noodles welcomed the moonless and dark sky. Noodles began to float with the flow of the river; he swam and swam until he was exhausted. Noodles was ready to quit when he tasted salt, he was home finally! Home to his beloved family, salt told Noodles that he was near Pattaya. Noodles made his way into the jungle to wait for the brilliant sunrise of Pattaya in the East that would rise over the gulf of Thailand. It seemed forever and was painfully slow; all he wanted to do was to go home and apologize to his parents.

Finally, there it was, the Sun, the brilliant morning Thai sun. There it was rising in the east. Noodles heart was pounding, now it would only be a matter of minutes before he would be reunited with his family. He began to slither away from the sun towards the horizon and the western part of Pattaya. The rocks that he remembered as breaking the calm of the ocean began to appear. Everything seemed more and more familiar until he knew he had reached home. Noodles now entered the jungle and as he approached the lair, he could make out his family, mother Teo, father Rama and the "little one," Lek. Noodles slithered as fast as he could to embrace mother Teo. As their scales rubbed against each other in a loving way and as their foreheads made contact, you could hear Noodles crying and asking for Moms forgiveness. Rama also embraced Noodles but he also proceeded to give him a stern lecture. Then it was Lek who wrapped herself around Noodles. The meeting of the scales was an unforgettable moment and Noodles now knew of the heartache that he had caused his family. Eventually all was forgiven and Noodles grew to a seven-foot strong Albino cobra, who is very obedient of family, respects all colors of snakes and is very appreciative of the wisdom of the old and will never forget the old python (Gupta) with the white beard and glasses who helped him escape the snake catchers. Noodles today has also made it a point to stay away from humans and the evil Mongoose.

Today Noodles takes life very seriously and appreciates every day of his life with his family.

The

End

Noodles Four Lessons Learned

1) We are all equal in the eyes of the creator, regardless of color or species.

2) Bullying—words can cause lasting mental anguish. Treat others as you would want to be treated.

3) Love your parents, be an obedient child. Your parents truly love you, you only have

one pair, and when they are gone, they are gone forever.

4) Respect the old as their wisdom is an accumulation from many years' experience.

Dedication

To all life, life is very precious. We must all learn to live together and share the only earth that we have, or we will all perish together. Live and let live and may peace be with you.

- Antonio Carnovale

Fact Sheet One

The Mongoose

- Mongooses are primarily found in Africa and Asia.

- There are 33 different types of mongoose with the smallest being the dwarf mongoose and the largest being the white tailed mongoose. The mongoose will eat rodents, snakes, birds, insects and some vegetation, fruit and nuts.

- The mongoose mostly lives in holes underground that have been vacated by other species. They also live in crevices on rocky areas.

- The mongoose can live to be 20 years old in captivity and as little as 4 yrs. old in the wild.

- The mongoose ranges in size from 7 inches long all the way up to 2 feet long.

- The mongoose has been introduced in different areas of the world in order to control the rodent population.

Fact Sheet Two

The Albino Cobra

- The Albino Cobra (Indian cobra) is found in India, Pakistan, and Southeast Asia.

- Average adult length is 6 feet long, but can grow to be as long as 8 feet.

- Albino cobra venom will paralyze muscles and if not treated properly will lead to respitory failure and cardiac arrest. Only a small percent of its bites are fatal and if untreated, the death rate is somewhere between 15-20%.

- In India, all cobras are revered. In Indian mythology, culture and are used by snake charmers.

- Cobras will eat small mammals, birds, frogs, rodents and other snakes.

- Albino cobras do not live long in the wild as they cannot camouflage themselves from their predators.

Printed in the United States
By Bookmasters